jE PEARSON Peter
How to walk a dump truck
/
Pearson, Peter,

WITHDRAWN
SEP 2 5 2019

D0709670

How To Walk a Dump Truck

For Kate, who loves all beings.
For Jupiter, who is not a dump truck.
And for someone I have not yet met. Welcome.
—P.P.

How to Walk a Dump Truck
Text copyright © 2019 by Peter Pearson
Illustrations copyright © 2019 by Mircea Catusanu
All rights reserved. Manufactured in China.
No part of this book may be used or reproduced in any manner whatsoever without
written permission except in the case of brief quotations embodied in critical
articles and reviews. For information address HarperCollins Children's Books,
a division of HarperCollins Publishers, 195 Broadway, New York, NY 10007.
www.harpercollinschildrens.com
ISBN 978-0-06-232063-6

The artist used Photoshop to create the digital illustrations for this book.

Typography by Rachel Zegar
19 20 21 22 23 SCP 10 9 8 7 6 5 4 3 2 1
❖
First Edition

WARNING TO KIDS: After reading this book, some grown-ups may try to park a full-sized
dump truck in your bedroom. Do not let them! It will smoosh your bed. And you.

HOW TO WALK A DUMP TRUCK

by Peter Pearson

illustrated by Mircea Catusanu

ONE WAY

HARPER

An Imprint of HarperCollins*Publishers*

Everyone knows that dump trucks make the best pets. However, adopting a dump truck is a big responsibility.

When choosing your dump truck, look for the one with a twinkle in its headlights and a rumble in its engine. You'll know when you've found your forever truck.

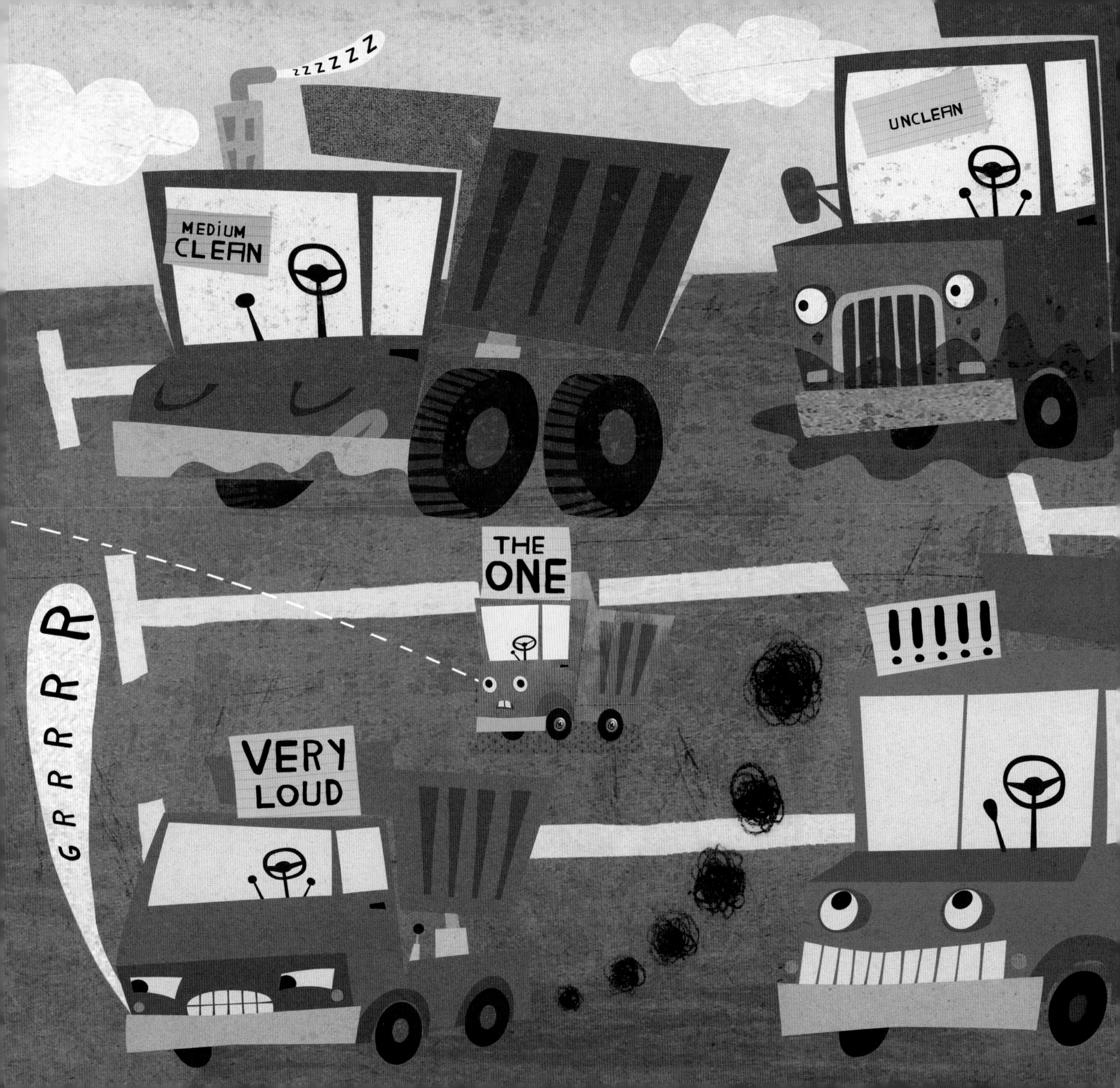
zzzzzZZ
MEDIUM CLEAN
UNCLEAN
THE ONE
GRRRRRRR
!!!!!
VERY LOUD

Once you bring it home, your dump truck will be eager to explore. Let it drive around your living room as it gets to know you. Some trucks are shy at first, but be patient. Every dump truck is full of love.

Dump trucks can't walk on an empty tank. Give it a good breakfast. Even small trucks can guzzle gas.

Before you can walk your dump truck, it needs a special tag called a license plate.

License plates tell you which truck belongs to whom. That way, if someone finds your truck, they will know whom to call.

DESIGNER BRAND

HEAVY DUTY

REAL LEATHER

Look for them in the truck section of the pet store. Leashes come in many sizes, so pick one that's right for your dump truck.

Now it's time for your walk. Clip the leash to the bumper so that your dump truck will walk beside you and not run into other trucks.

A new truck has a lot of energy, so be sure to walk it around two or three hundred blocks.

Don't be surprised if your truck likes to honk. It might honk at squirrels, birds, people, other trucks, shadows, the sky, or nothing. If your dump truck honks too much, say "No!" in a firm voice.

When it stops, pat it on the hood and give it a treat. This will help it learn to behave.

while on your walk, go to places that trucks enjoy, like construction sites.

Another fun spot is the truck park. Bring a friend!
Dump trucks love romping with other vehicles.
Plus, it's a great way to burn fuel.

Of course, dump trucks love the dump. Play a round of "Haul the Dirt" or "Fetch the Boulder." Dump trucks are especially good at "Make a Pile."

If your dump truck
makes a pile, though,
be sure to clean it up.
Sometimes a shovel will
work, but for bigger piles,
ask a backhoe for help.

Most dump trucks adore the water.
Take them to the lake for a swim.

See who makes the biggest splash!

Your truck will be very dirty after playing all day.
Walk it home and wash it in the driveway.

First, scrub the wheels. Then wash the pistons. Don't forget to dry the doors and windows of the cab, where the seats are. Clean trucks are happy trucks!

1-Scrub

2-Wash

3-Dry

4-Happy!

once your truck is dry, it's time to say good-bye.

Your dump truck will want to play all night, but don't let it fool you. Its tank will be almost empty.

your bed.

You'll both need your rest for later . . .

. . . when it grows up.

HONK!
HONK!
HONK!
OVERSIZE LOAD
ONE WAY
ARKANSAS
TRUCK
A GR8-K9
EXP. 04 01 20

Quiz: Dog or Dump Truck?

Most people can't tell the difference between dogs and dump trucks. Can you?

QUESTION: Most of my kind dump out the back, but some dump out the side or even out the bottom. Dog or dump truck?

ANSWER: Dump truck! Just like dogs, there are different kinds of dump trucks. Many of them tip up and dump out the back. However, a side dump truck is long and tips sideways, which unloads much faster. A bottom dump truck has doors that open in the floor of the dump box. This lets them lay their load out in a long row instead of a big heap.

QUESTION: I am one of the fastest land animals on earth. I am also very cuddly. Dog or dump truck?

ANSWER: Dog! Greyhounds can hit their top speed of forty-five miles per hour in only six steps. The only animal that can do it faster is the cheetah. Greyhounds are also the oldest dog breed in the world. You can see them in images from ancient Egypt and Greece.

QUESTION: I'm a smaller version of my species called a "pup." I follow the bigger ones around and love to carry stuff. I am very adorable. Dog or dump truck?

ANSWER: Trick question! It's both! Young dogs are called puppies (or pups, for short), but "pup" is also the name of a small trailer hauled behind some dump trucks. The dump truck's load is put into the pup, which makes several trips to the work site so the dump truck doesn't have to go as far.

QUESTION: I can hear and smell way, way better than you, but you win at seeing and tasting. Dog or dump truck?

ANSWER: Dog! Dogs can hear four times farther than people can, but their noses are the real champions. A dog's sense of smell is at least ten thousand times better than a human's. Specially trained dogs can even tell if someone has cancer just by sniffing their breath. People have more sensitive eyes and tongues, though, which is why dogs eat gross stuff sometimes. They can't taste it as well as you can.

QUESTION: I love being outside. Yards are my favorite! Dog or dump truck?

ANSWER: Another trick question! It's both! Dogs love being outside in the yard, but "yard" is also a way of measuring how much a dump truck can carry. A cubic yard is a box three feet on each side. A regular dump truck can carry ten to fourteen yards. The biggest dump trucks can carry more than two hundred yards.

QUESTION: Sometimes exhaust flows through my floor to heat it up. Dog or dump truck?

ANSWER: Dump truck! Fumes that come from the engine are very hot, so some dump trucks use that heat to make their loads slide out more easily.

QUESTION: I have eight wheels and two engines and am as big as a house. Dog or dump truck?

ANSWER: Dump truck! The BelAZ 75710 is the biggest dump truck in the world. It's so big that the driver has to go up a flight of stairs just to get inside. The wheels alone are thirteen feet tall. This dump truck can haul almost a million pounds of rock, which is more than seven hundred classrooms of first graders! It's also far too big to drive on normal roads. To move to a new job site, it has to be taken apart and put back together.

QUESTION: If you looked at my nose up close, you wouldn't find another like it in the entire world. Dog or dump truck?

ANSWER: Dog! The nose print of a dog is unique, just like human fingerprints. No two are alike, and you can use them to tell dogs apart.

BelAZ 75710

WASHINGTON 954·ZDX

How did you do?

ALL THE ANSWERS RIGHT: Dr. Trucks

You definitely know the difference between dogs and dump trucks! Whenever you see a truck, you say, "That right there is a truck, not a dog." Well done.

MOST OF THE ANSWERS RIGHT: Dog Mechanic

Rare is the time you don't know what's a dump truck and what's a dog. It may have only happened once, and you were probably sleepy. Good job!

SOME OF THE ANSWERS RIGHT: Truck-Dog Fan

When your mom asks you to get a dump truck from the store, sometimes you come home with a poodle instead. But don't worry! You can improve!

NONE OF THE ANSWERS RIGHT: Truck Dump

Looks like you need some practice! Ask a friend to put a dog and a dump truck next to each other. The differences are subtle, but you'll notice them if you look hard. (Hint: The dog is the one without tires.) Good luck! You can do it!